# LOTTIE'S CATS

Written by
Mirabel Cecil

Illustrated by
Francesca Martin

WALKER BOOKS
LONDON

Lottie was an only child but she was never lonely. Instead of brothers and sisters for company, she had cats.

They all lived in a hut in the garden. At least, Lottie lived there most of the time; she didn't always sleep there because her mother said that her bed indoors was more comfortable. But in summer Lottie took her sleeping bag to the hut at night. She lay awake as long as she could and watched the stars come out. In winter she played inside the hut while the snowflakes softly covered it in white, or the rain pattered on the roof.

Lottie loved her hut: on the walls she put up the pictures she had done at school. Outside, she sowed seeds – sunflowers, marigolds and cornflowers – to make her own special garden.

Whenever other children from school came to play, Lottie didn't go into her hut but waited until they had gone home.

Lottie had a cat for every day of the week:

Monday's cat had a sumptuous black and white tail of which she was immensely proud; she swished it about from side to side as she walked.

Tuesday's cat had almost no tail since the time he crossed the road without looking both ways and a car ran over it. (He was always very careful how he crossed the road after that.)

Wednesday's cat was given to Lottie by the old lady next door who had more cats than she could cope with. He had a huge appetite and liked at least three meals a day, with snacks in between.

Thursday's cat was Siamese: she had lots to say, especially at night when Lottie's mum had to shoo her away; then she stalked down the garden path to the hut on her silvery paws, her tail held proudly upright.

Friday's cat was a magic cat. At least Lottie thought so from the moment she first saw him. That was one summer night, when Lottie looked out of her bedroom window. She saw the moon, full and bright, move from behind the clouds and then she saw the cat – a beautiful white cat, dancing alone on the lawn.

Lottie's mother said it must have been a dream – but in the morning when Lottie went out to her hut, there he was, and she invited him in. Lottie's mother said he must be a stray, but Lottie knew better. When she stroked Friday's cat little sparks seemed to come out of his fur. At night, his slanting green eyes glittered like stars. Lottie's mother said that all cats' eyes glow in the dark, but Lottie knew better.

He slept curled up beside her and she was sure that he gave her good dreams. He was a cat with a lot of secrets.

Lottie loved all her cats but Friday's cat she loved most of all.

Then there was Saturday, Lottie's youngest cat. She was just a kitten, small and fluffy, with a soft wet nose. The others taught her where to sharpen her claws on the walls of the hut and how to catch flies in the sunshine. Sunday's cat was the oldest of them all. His legs were a bit stiff and he had a big, baggy shape. He was Lottie's first kitten and so became her chief of cats.

Lottie often read to her cats inside the hut. Sometimes they listened, sometimes they went to sleep. Tuesday's cat always listened carefully: he liked to hear adventure stories about cats going for long voyages on board ships. Wednesday's cat only liked stories about food; he rubbed himself against Lottie and purred, hoping it would soon be time for another meal.

"If you purr so loudly, you won't be able to hear the story," Lottie said.

So now you can see why Lottie was so happy in her hut with all her cats – until the terrible day when Friday's cat disappeared. The day before he vanished, he ate a much bigger breakfast and supper than usual but he refused to come into the hut. Instead, he curled up in a nest he had made for himself. And the next day, when Lottie went to say goodbye to him before she went to school, he was nowhere to be seen. Lottie looked all over the garden but there was no sign of Friday's cat.

"Come along or you'll be late for school," said Lottie's mother. "Cats often go missing for a few days. He'll soon be back."

But when Lottie returned, Friday's cat was still missing. "Friday, Friday..." she called anxiously. Then she and the rest of her cats set off to search the neighbourhood.

Saturday's kitten jumped on to the wall to look in next door's garden. She almost fell trying to get back and Lottie had to rescue her.

"Stay with me!" she told her. "We don't want both of you lost." So the kitten snuggled down in Lottie's cardigan and the two of them searched together.

Sunday's cat perched on the roof of the hut from where he could look into other houses.

Monday's cat carefully searched the old lady's garden.

She stopped to look at her reflection in a little pond and this gave her great pleasure.

Tuesday's cat climbed the tallest tree he knew. He got a bit frightened when the branches began to sway, but he carried on boldly to the very top.

Wednesday's cat miaowed outside the old lady's kitchen window, while Thursday's cat made several stops along the garden walls, yowling as loudly as she possibly could at every one.

But there was no answer.

Lottie's mum pinned up a notice:

LARGE REWARD FOR FINDING
A BEAUTIFUL WHITE CAT

Monday's cat thought he might have been eaten by a huge dog.

Remembering what had happened to *him*, Tuesday's cat wondered whether he had been run over and squashed by a car.

Wednesday's cat thought he might have been locked in someone's garden shed by mistake.

Thursday's cat trembled to think that he might have climbed a tall tree and be unable to get down again.

Sunday's cat was afraid that he had been stolen because he was so beautiful.

Saturday's kitten squeaked excitedly – she thought she saw him! But it was only dead leaves blown by the breeze.

"Don't cry," said Lottie, gently stroking her. "I know he'll come back."

CAT

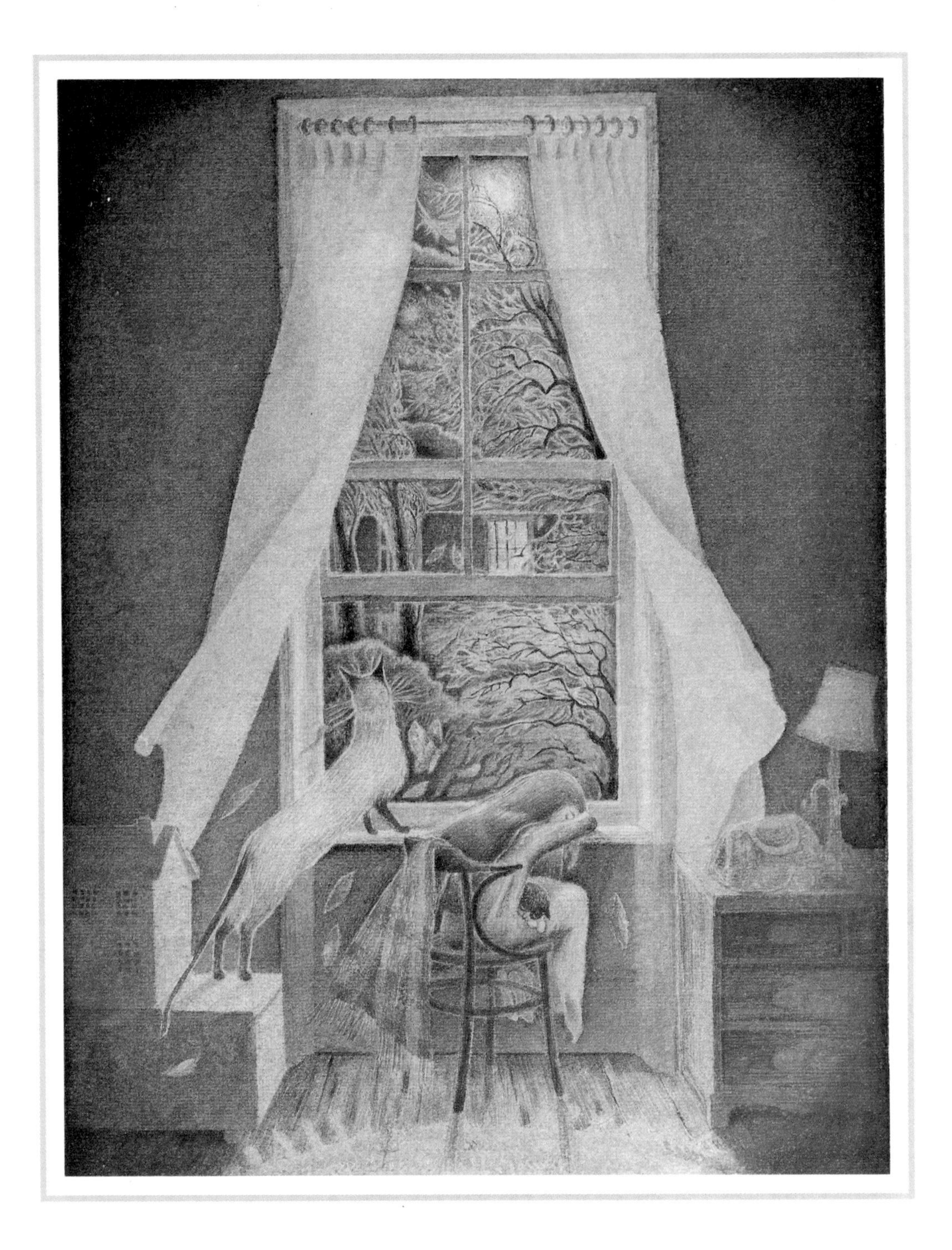

But would he? Every night for seven nights Lottie watched from her bedroom window, hoping to see Friday's cat dancing in the moonlight, as she had first seen him. But the only movement outside was from the shadows of the bare branches tossing in the wind. For hours she sat gazing out at the empty garden while the tears trickled down her cold cheeks.

Thursday's cat kept watch with her. For once, she had very little to say but she mewed softly to comfort Lottie. Saturday's kitten dried Lottie's tears with her little pink tongue.

Eventually, Lottie got into bed and the kitten snuggled up beside her.

Every morning Lottie said to herself: "Today, I *know* Friday's cat will come back." But seven more days passed and still there was no sign of him.

The next evening was Hallowe'en. To cheer her up, Lottie's mother suggested that she take her supper out to the hut. But Lottie didn't want to go to her hut; nor did she want any supper. Wednesday's cat, who could always fit in an extra meal, ate it instead.

Lottie went slowly upstairs to bed but no matter how hard she tried, she couldn't seem to go to sleep.

Outside, the stars shone dimly. Great clouds swirled across the sky. Strange shapes fled before the moon, which was fuller and brighter than ever. It seemed to Lottie that suddenly a brilliant shape came whirling down out of the sky, nearer and nearer, its brightness filling the air as she watched from the window.

Lottie felt that she simply must run downstairs and out into the garden.

Lottie was just in time to see Friday's cat jump down from the sky. In an instant it was all dark again – except for the sparkling fur of Friday's cat and his strange, starry-bright eyes.

Then Friday's cat danced for Lottie in the garden.

"So you *are* a magic cat!" she whispered, hugging him close.

In the morning, it wasn't her mother who woke Lottie as usual, nor the ringing of her alarm clock, but the rough tongue of Friday's cat gently licking her face.

When Lottie told her mother about how he had returned, she just laughed kindly and said it was a dream; Friday's cat must have got lost and managed to find his own way back.

But Lottie knew better.

"Next time you go away," Lottie said,
looking into his gleaming eyes,
"can we *all* come with you?"